This Little Tiger book belongs to:

_____

_____

_____

For Charlie and Billy with love
~ M C B

For Amelia Bahrani
~ T M

LITTLE TIGER PRESS
1 The Coda Centre, 189 Munster Road, London SW6 6AW
www.littletigerpress.com

First published in Great Britain 2012
This edition published 2013
Text copyright © M Christina Butler 2012
Illustrations copyright © Tina Macnaughton 2012

A CIP catalogue record for this book is available from the British Library

All rights reserved • ISBN 978-1-84895-309-3

Printed in China • LTP/1800/0533/0113

2 4 6 8 10 9 7 5 3 1

Mouse
and the
Moon

M Christina Butler

Illustrated by Tina Macnaughton

LITTLE TIGER PRESS
London

Little Harvest Mouse lived by himself at the top of the corn. Every night, the warm summer breezes rocked his cosy nest, and his friend the moon watched over him from the deep blue sky.

Before Little Harvest Mouse closed his
eyes each night, he sang a lullaby to his
very own moon.

But one evening, a cold wind rustled
through the corn and Little Harvest
Mouse couldn't see his friend anywhere.

Little Harvest Mouse peeked out of his nest.
Everything looked so different without the moon's
friendly glow.

Trembling, he raced through the corn
and across the meadow. "Someone's stolen
the moon!" he shouted at the
top of his voice.

"Stolen the moon?" quacked Duck. "I can't believe that! The moon will be in the pond where she always is."

"In the pond?" thought Little Harvest Mouse. "That can't be!" But he followed Duck as she looked in the water . . .

The moon was not there.

"Where has she gone?" cried Duck.

"The moon doesn't live in the pond!" laughed Squirrel, who was listening nearby. "She's above my nest in the fir tree."

"The moon doesn't live in a tree!" sniffed Duck.

"She does!" said Squirrel.
He scampered round every
branch, but he couldn't
find the moon.

"She's not here!" he called
down in a panic. "The
wind must have blown
her away!"

Hare was on his way home when he heard all the fuss.

"Blown the moon away?" he grinned. "Never! She was with me when I ran to the mountains."

"The moon doesn't go to the mountains!" said Squirrel.

"Of course she does!" cried Hare. So they all dashed after him to find the moon.

Little Harvest Mouse searched the sky. Duck looked
in every pool and puddle. Squirrel scrambled in and out
of the trees, and Hare bounded high and low. But they
couldn't find the moon anywhere.
As the wind blew stronger, thunder
rumbled round the hills.

"What have you done with my moon, Squirrel?"
snapped Duck.

"It's not your moon, it's mine!" Squirrel cried.
"Anyway, Hare must have lost her!"

"I've done no such thing!" grumbled Hare.

"But what shall I do without her?" squeaked
Little Harvest Mouse. "I'll be all alone!"

FLASH! BOOM! Lightning lit up the sky.
  CRACK! CRASH! Thunder clattered over the mountains.
  "Follow me!" shouted Hare. "I know where there's a cave!"

They
raced
through
the storm
and squeezed
together in
the cave.

"I'm sorry I snapped," whispered Duck.

"It was my fault," Squirrel piped up. "I shouldn't have blamed Hare."

"No harm done," said Hare bravely. And as the storm raged on they told each other stories.

At last, the rain stopped and the clouds rumbled away.

"Look! Look!" cried Little Harvest Mouse.
The clear dark sky was full of twinkling stars,
and peeping out from amongst them was the moon!
It was glowing brightly over the mountains . . .
glittering through the trees . . .
and shining in the pond . . .

"The same moon belongs to us all,"
whispered Duck.
"She never really left us," said Squirrel.
"Good friends never do," nodded Hare wisely.
"And best of all," smiled Little Harvest Mouse,
"she's given me three new friends!"

More wonderful books from Little Tiger Press . . .

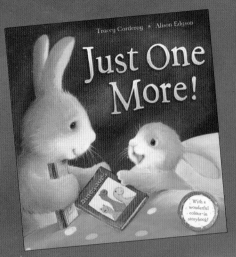

Tracey Corderoy * Alison Edgson

Just One More!

With a wonderful colour-in storybook!

A touch-and-feel book

One Special Day

M Christina Butler * Tina Macnaughton

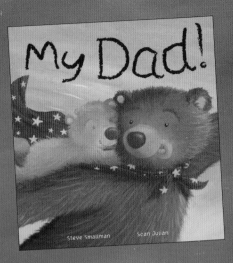

My Dad!

Steve Smallman * Sean Julian

Steve Smallman * Hannah George

Dr DUCK

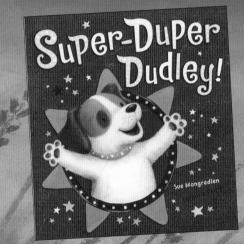

Super-Duper Dudley!

Sue Mongredien

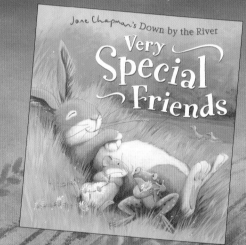

Jane Chapman's Down by the River

Very Special Friends

For information regarding any of the above titles
or for our catalogue, please contact us:
Little Tiger Press, 1 The Coda Centre,
189 Munster Road, London SW6 6AW
Tel: 020 7385 6333 • Fax: 020 7385 7333
E-mail: info@littletiger.co.uk
www.littletigerpress.com